W9-BIA-732

J PAR STORYTIME KIT BOD

Bodies [storytime kit]
Total - 22 pieces

WITHDRAWN

Busy Toes

Busy Toes

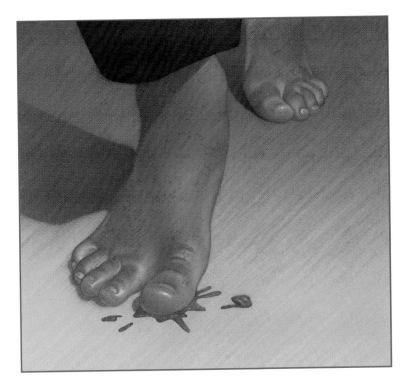

by C. W. Bowie

illustrated by

Fred Willingham

ROCKFORD PUBLIC LIBRARY

Whispering Coyote
A Charlesbridge Imprint

For my husband, who always knew I'd be published one day
—W.O.

Although all eleven of my grandchildren have very busy toes, I dedicate this
book especially to Haley and Jackson Eargle and Michael McGonigle
—M. B-K.

To my father, Count Gibson, who taught me to write with my toes
—C.G.W.

To my girls, Desirée and Nikkia
—F.W.

A **Whispering Coyote** Book
First paperback edition 2002
Text copyright © 1998 by C. W. Bowie
Illustrations copyright © 1998 by Fred Willingham
All rights reserved including the right of reproduction in whole or in part in any form.
Charlesbridge, Whispering Coyote, and colophon are registered trademarks of Charlesbridge Publishing.

Published by Charlesbridge Publishing
85 Main Street
Watertown, MA 02472
www.charlesbridge.com

Library of Congress Cataloging-in-Publication Data
Bowie, C. W.
Busy toes / written by C. W. Bowie ; illustrated by Fred Willingham
p. cm.
Summary: A playful list of some of the many things that toes can do, from
waving and tickling to tasting and dancing.
ISBN 1–879085–72–0 (reinforced for library use)
ISBN 1–58089–081-4 (softcover)
[1. Toes—Fiction. 2. Stories in rhyme.] I. Title.
PZ8.3.B677Bu 1997
[E]—dc20 96–30588
CIP
AC

Printed in China
(hc) 10 9 8 7 6 5 4 3 2 1
(sc) 10 9 8 7 6 5 4 3 2 1

Text was set in 30-point Goudy Bold.
Book production and design by *The Kids at Our House*

BIG TOES,

little toes

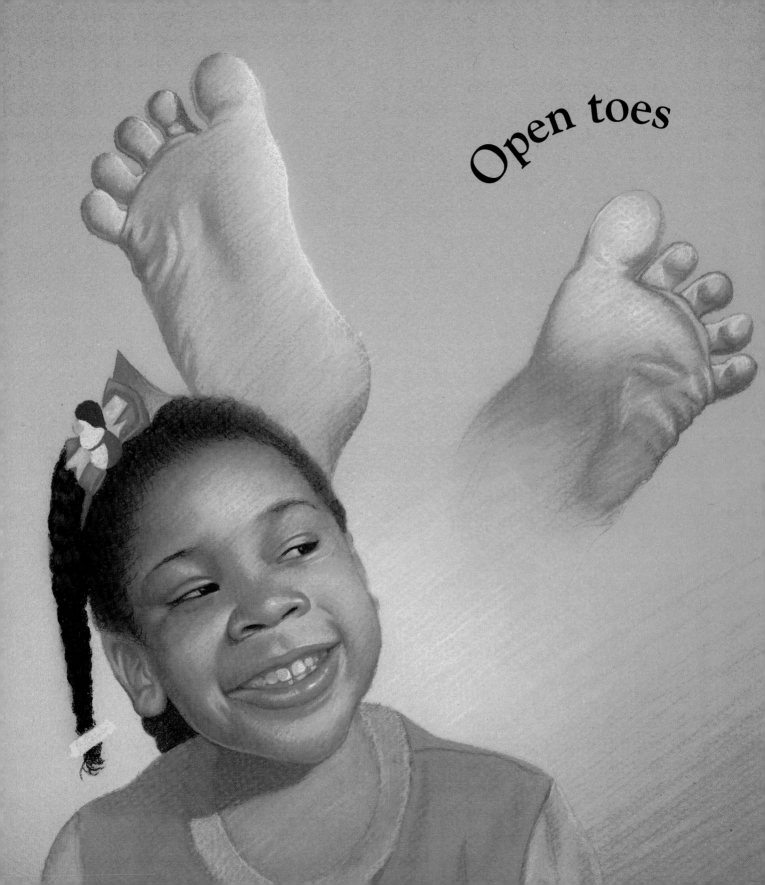

Open toes

And closed toes

Waving toes

Tickling toes

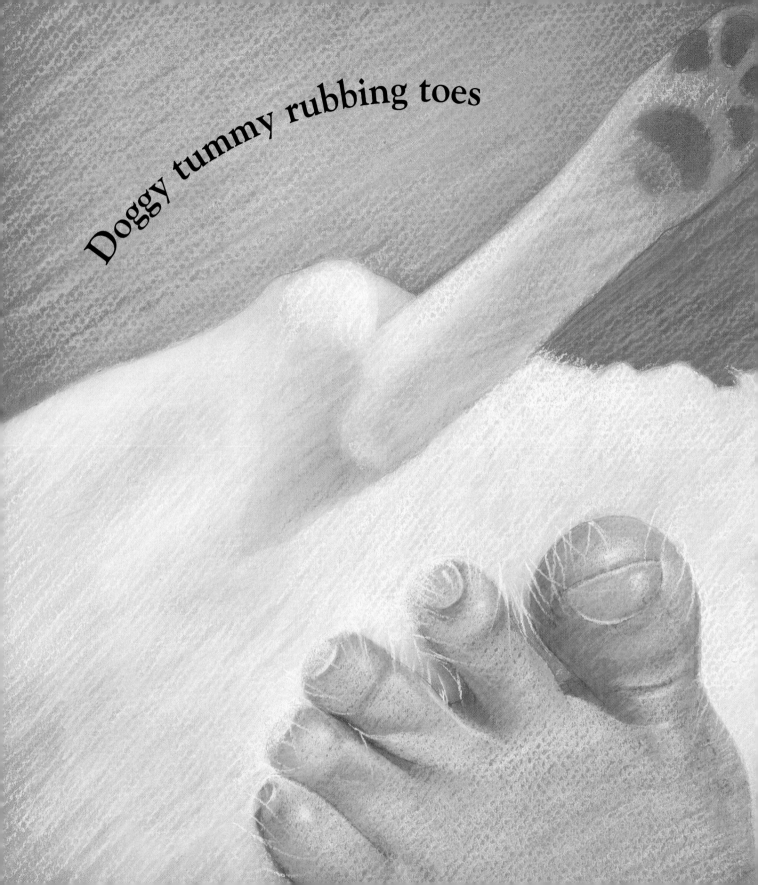

Doggy tummy rubbing toes

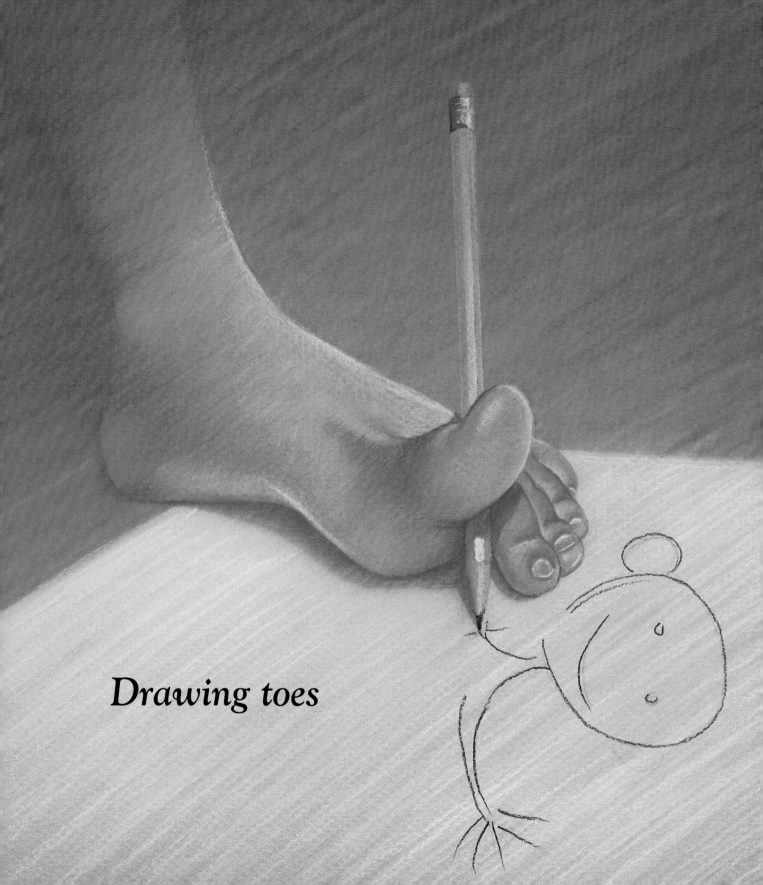

Drawing toes

Digging toes

Hidden toes

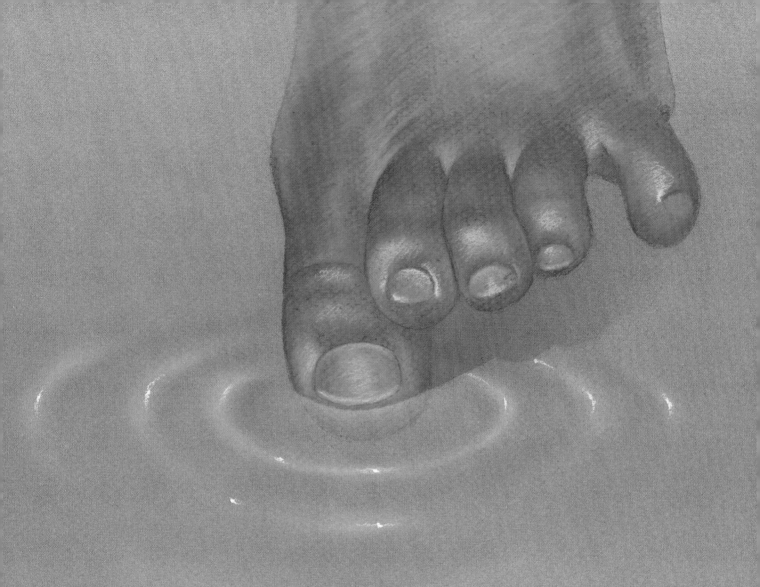

Testing toes

Splashing toes

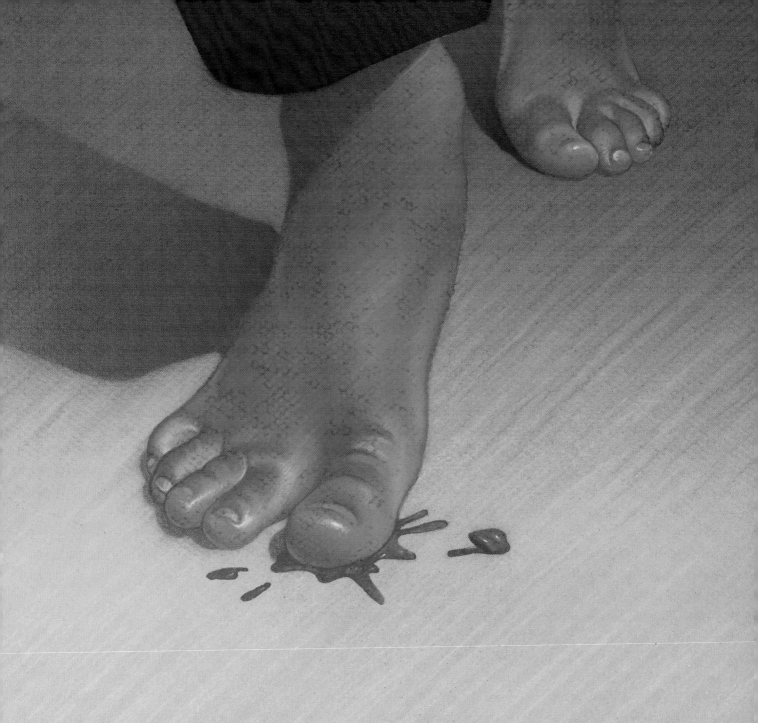

Squishing toes

And don't forget
the fishing toes

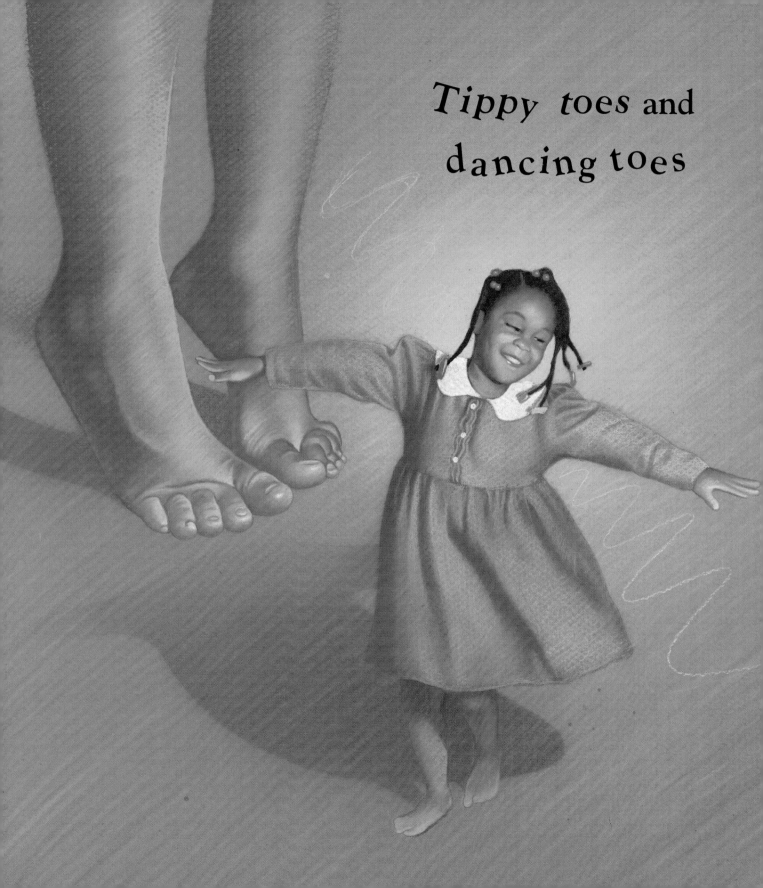

Tippy toes and
dancing toes

Tasting toes

Counting toes

1

2

3

Pick-up toes

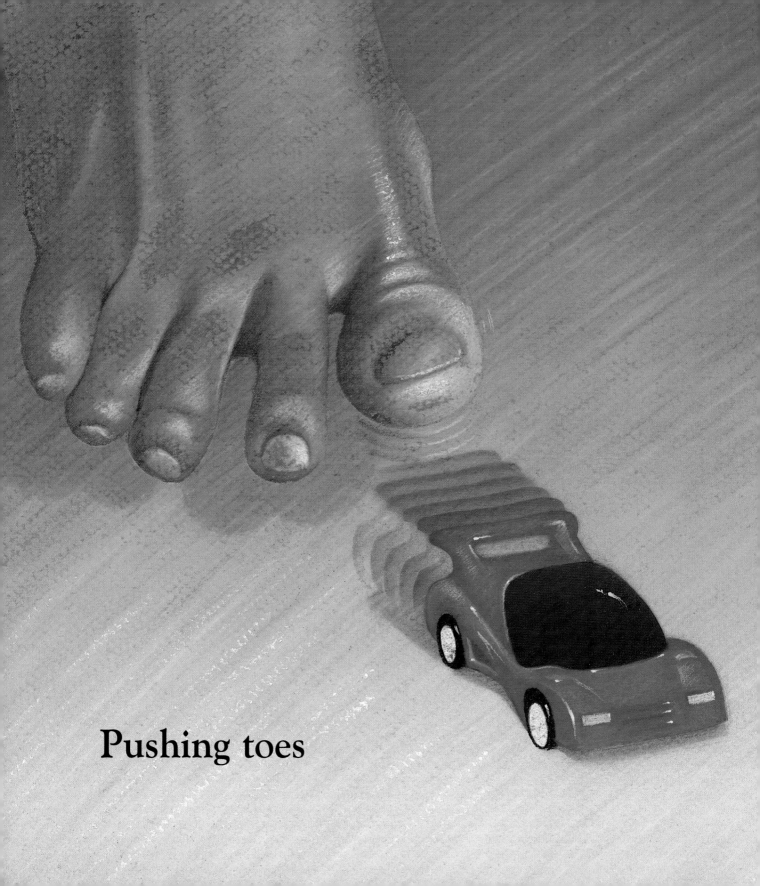

Pushing toes

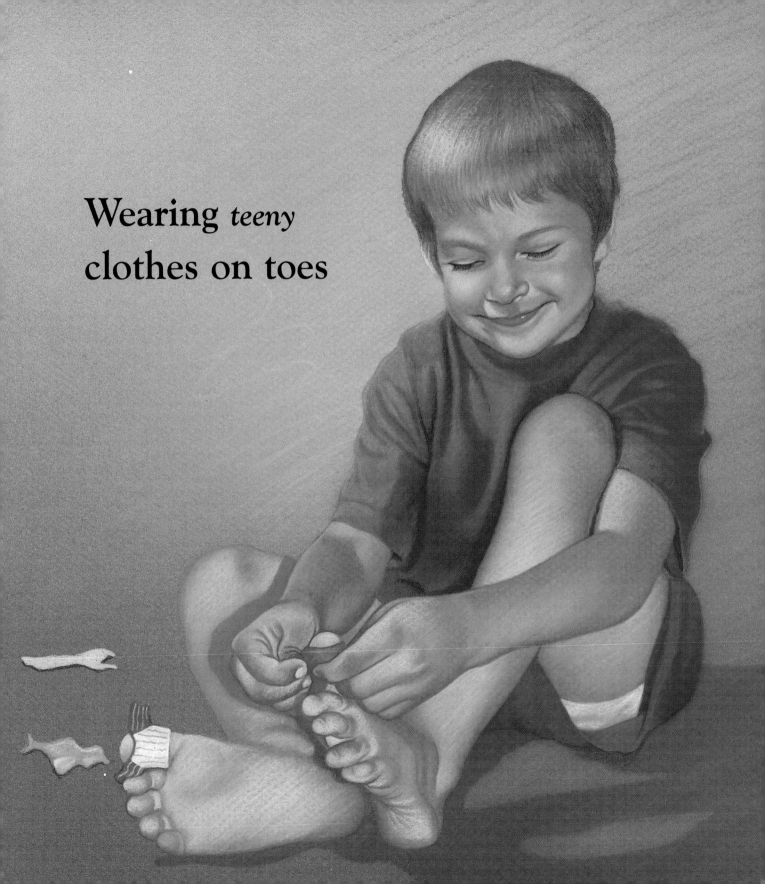

Wearing *teeny*
clothes on toes

Soapy toes

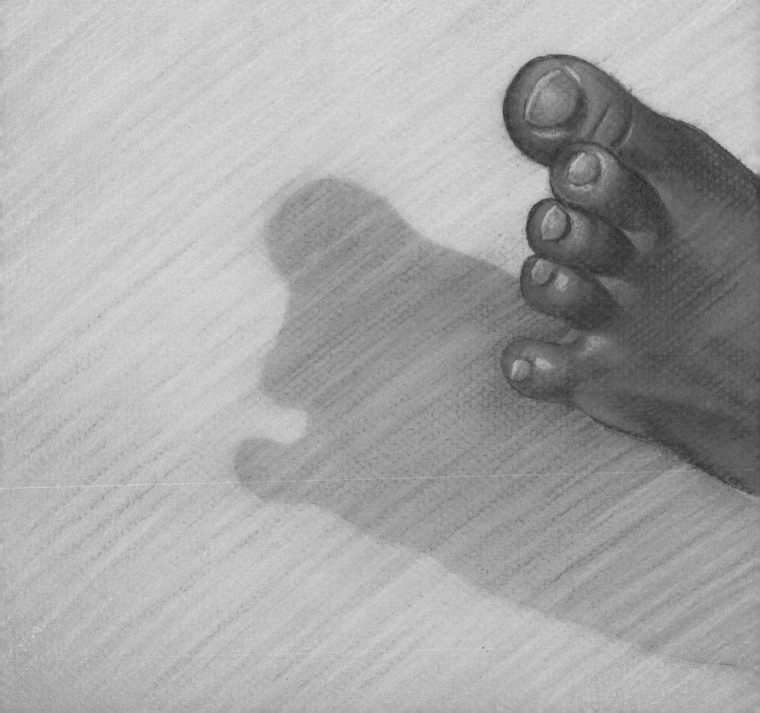

Shadow toes

Tired toes

And tent toes

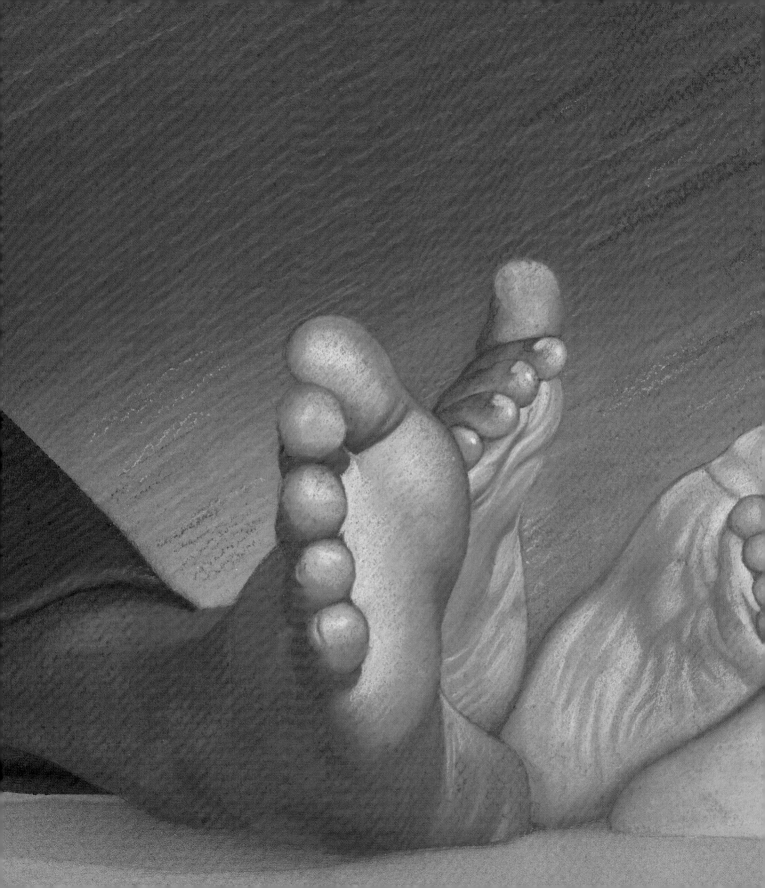

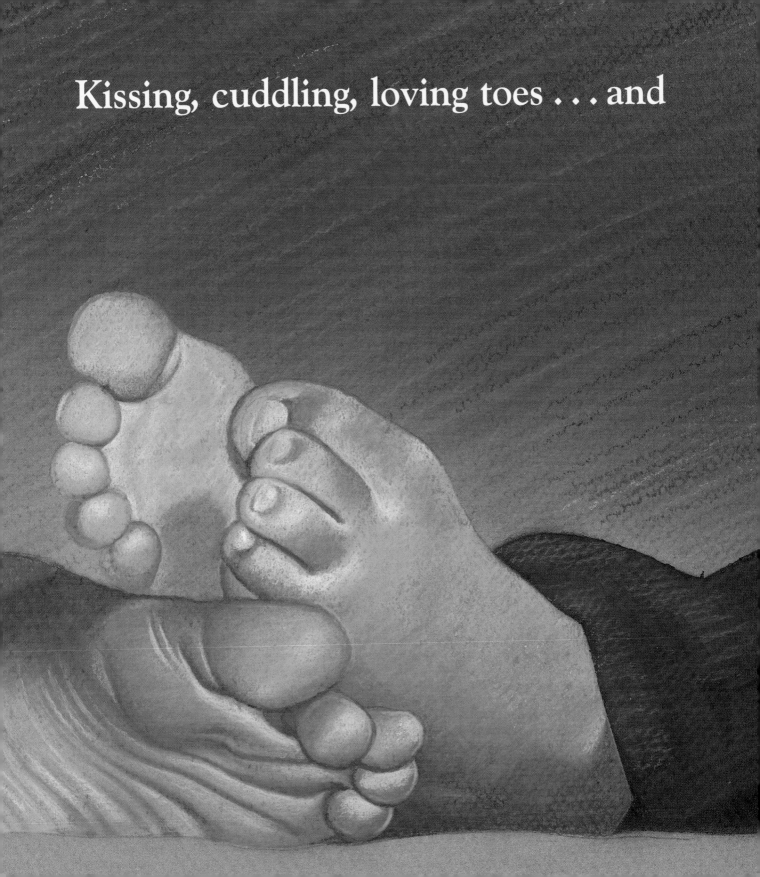

Kissing, cuddling, loving toes ... and

Goodnight, toes!